Ging Gang Goolie, It's An Alien

Bob Wilson

Young Lions

Published in Young Lions 1988
Tenth impression May 1993

Young Lions is an imprint of the Children's Division,
part of HarperCollins Publishers Ltd,
77–85 Fulham Palace Road, Hammersmith, London W6 8JB

Copyright © 1988 Bob Wilson

Printed and bound in Great Britain by
HarperCollins Manufacturing, Glasgow

THIS IS GARRY WIMBUSH.

He is a Boy Scout.

And on the particular Friday night
which begins this story, he is a
rather excited Boy Scout.
For next morning he and the rest
of his scout-troop are going off
to camp.

We're going to
Blackbank woods,
YEEE.... HAH!

Skip, the scout-leader, had
issued them with a list of the kit
that they should take to camp:

 3RD BALSALWOOD RD
SCOUT TROOP

These are the essential items of equipment
you should bring to camp :-

Sleeping-bag.
Ground-sheet. (Heavy duty)
Torch.
Compass (Army type)
Whistle.
Boots. (Or stout walking-shoes)
Soap, Towel, Toothbrush.
Knife, fork and spoon.
Penknife.
Needle & thread.
Billy-can.
Mug and plate. (<u>Tin</u> - not the best China!)
<u>Matches</u>

Skip

Garry's mother had made
a list too:

Dont forget

Warm Woolie vests
Slippers.
Hot water bottle (Teddybear?)
Wooly cardigan
Wooly hat
pyjamas & dressing gown
Talcum powder
Calamine Lotion
Soft toilet Roll ← (Tell him to
                    wash his hands)
Aspirins, hand cream.
comb & hairbrush.
* Matches ← (Tell him to be carefull)
Wooly mittens

So had Garry:

things what I must'tnt
forget For camp.   SKIP ↓

MARS BARS
   chewing gum
CATERPULT
    marbles
      PEASHOOTER
CHOCLATE BISCITS ← (Lots)
COMICS ←
MATCHES ←   For bonfiRES
         DONT FORGET!
mouth-ORGAN   Cpt marvel.
Pet frog ← If mum'L Let me.
PLAYiN CARDS
SPUD-gun
BAGS OF CRISPS
FIND WOGGLE

PEN NIFE.

And so, on that Friday night, his mum was helping him to pack. Garry, as usual, lost his woggle.

His mum lost her temper.

And by 9 o'clock they'd both lost their presence of mind.

But eventually the job was done and by 10 o'clock Garry was tucked up in bed.

The motto of the Boy Scouts is:

BE PREPARED

And Garry slept soundly that night thinking that, like a good boy scout, he was prepared for anything.

He was prepared for swimming,
climbing, and leaky tents.
He was prepared for snowstorms,
heat waves, and floods.
He was prepared for chilblains,
sunburn, and midge bites.

But what he was not
    prepared for was . . .

THE INVASION OF THE GROBBLE.

---

1. The Grobblewockians are a race of **Alien space Monsters!** They live on the planet GROB which is millions of billions of squillions of miles away. So far away that nobody has ever been there because by the time they got halfway, it would be time to come back.

2. Nobody on Earth has ever heard of a Grobblewockian . . .

So I'd better tell you something
about them . . .

3. The average Grobblewockian is not all that different from the average rather ugly Earthman.*
But Grobblewockians <u>are</u> unlike the average Earthman in a number of ways.

Hand ⇦

knee ⇨

⇦ Bumper Daisy

✱ (Take a good look at your father.)

For example:
Grobblewockians don't watch 'Top of the Pops'.

Grobblewockians love sausages.

But, above all, Grobblewockians are incredibly . . . .

4. It was a Grobblewockian alien named Orrice Dee-orrible who invented the most evil weapon in the universe:

◄o THE GROBBLEWOCKIAN LASER RAY·GUN o►

Grobblifier

knoblifier

Wobblifier

For example:
If you were to point a Grobblewockian laser ray-gun at a whole circus tent full of clowns, strongmen, tigers, lions, trapeze artists, conjurors, bandsmen, zebras, performing seals, ringmasters, fire eaters, jugglers and small children eating ice-creams . . . and then pull the trigger!
This is what would happen.

15

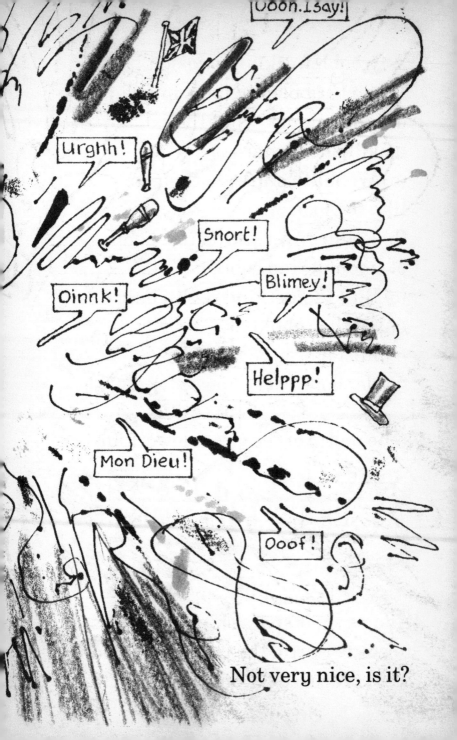

5. A Grobblewockian invasion:
When Grobblewockians invade
another planet, what they
usually do is this –

(a) Wobblify anybody they don't
like the look of.

(b) Reduce everything to a heap
of smouldering rubble.

(c) Build something really ugly
out of the rubble like
a multi-storey car-park or
a telephone exchange. ✳ ↗

6. The motto of the Grobblewockians is:

BEE PREE ! PEAR HEAD

And as their space ship moved closer
towards Earth, the Grobblewockians
were prepared for anything.

*(Why they should want to do this no one really knows, but it has been said that the brain of the average alien monster is not all that different from the brain of the average football hooligan or a brick.

The brain of a football hooligan

A Brick

A peanut

DIAGRAM 1.

They were prepared for evil, terror and nastiness.
They were prepared for fire, pestilence, and storm.
They were prepared for wizards, ghouls, and football hooligans.

But what they were
        not prepared for was . . .

KEY TO DIAGRAM 2.

A Tich   E Iggy   I Specs

B Loopy   F Darren   J Bazzer

C Studge   G Garry   K Willis

D Nobby   H Skip   L Fred

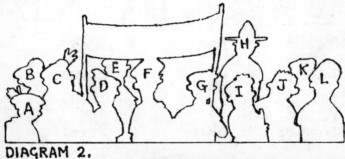

DIAGRAM 2.

Now back to the story.

On Saturday morning at 10 o'clock
Garry met up with the rest of the
troop outside the scout-hut.
Skip gave them their orders:

We shall march to the campsite.
I have worked out our best route
using this map and compass.
It should take us about 30 minutes.
Right boys. Follow me.

THE MARCH TO THE CAMPSITE

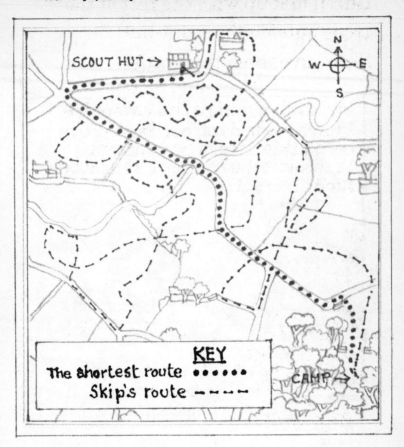

SCOUT HUT →

KEY

The shortest route •••••

Skip's route – – – –

CAMP →

When they got to the camp-site
Skip said:

Half-past four.
Not bad going.
Right. First we'll have...
......kit Inspection.

Have you all brought....
sleeping-bag, ground-sheet,
torch, compass, and whistle?

Yes Skip.

Skip said not to worry. They would just have to use their ingenuity.

Darren Twigg said:

I haven't brought any ingenuity with me, Skip! It wasn't on the list.

Skip made a comment about
Darren Twigg's brain . . .

A CABBAGE

Then he explained that ingenuity
meant that they'd have to <u>think</u>
<u>hard</u> of another way to light a fire.

But first, he said, they must pitch
the tents.

A NOTE FROM THE AUTHOR :-

There are a number of methods
which can be used to pitch
a tent.
Over the page you will find
two of them :—

A. The correct method
B. The Balsawood Rd method

A) The correct method.

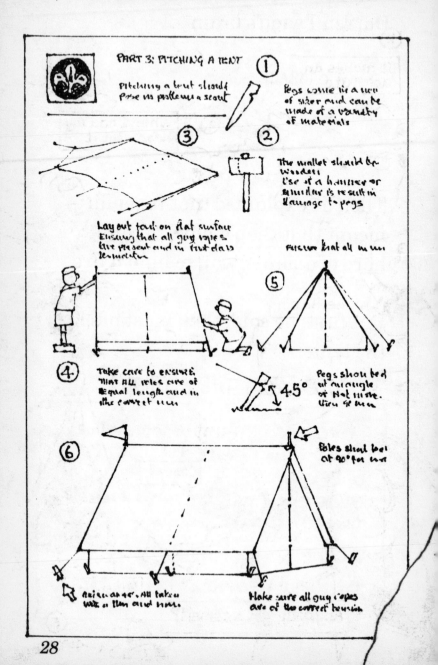

PART 3: PITCHING A TENT

① Pitching a tent should pose no problems a scout

Pegs come in a run of sizes and can be made of a variety of materials

③ Lay out tent on flat surface Ensuring that all guy ropes are present and in first class condition

② The mallet should be wooden Use of a hammer or similar is result in damage to pegs

④ Take care to ensure that all poles are of equal length and in the correct run

⑤ Ensure that all in run

45° Pegs should be at an angle of not more than 45 men

⑥ Poles should be at 90° for use

Raise an 45°. All taken with a item and run.

Make sure all guy ropes are of the correct tension

B) The Balsawood Rd. method

When the tents were up, everyone sat round in a circle, and Skip explained what their first test would be.

Skip made another comment about
Darren Twigg's brain . . .

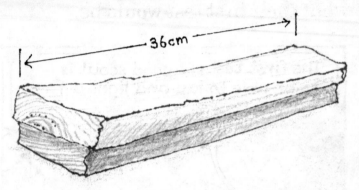

Then he went on to explain that
out of doors meant 'outside', and
that seeing as they'd forgotten the
matches, they would have to light a
fire by rubbing two pieces of wood
together.
This sounded like fun.
So they all ran off into the woods
to find some good sticks.
(N.B. It was while he was doing this
that Garry Wimbush lost his woggle.)

On board a Grobblewockian
space ship . . .

plans were being made.

A NOTE FROM THE AUTHOR

You may be thinking :-

"If these aliens come from a planet that's millions of trillions of squillions of miles away.... how come they speak perfect English?"

Well, the answer is ... 'They don't.' If I wrote down what they said in alien language you wouldn't understand - would you!

I'll do the last two pages again so that you can see what I mean

TAKE 2. ⇩

Dooyer finkaz wot deez Erf peepull goanta givus lotta assul?

Beet smee, Bigg-boz. Day cudbee ded bigg an orribull.

Wee-ort zend sum won ter fine dowt
Soze wee orl doant get kilt.

FINX :- Iffy finx azwot
Iam dafter-nuff ter
vol unt-ear —
— eeze gorra
nuver fink cummin.

Owazabout zend-in Alien Grott?
Eez az fick az too-shore-t'planx.

Worra
brilide ear!

See. You didn't understand a word
of that, did you?
You did!?
Oh well then, I might as well carry
on like that —

BACK TO THE STORY -(a bit later.)

Alien Grott sat at the controls of
the scout-ship. He was not due to
blast-off until 9 o'clock, Earthtime,
and he was getting bored.

Idly he looked out of the porthole
at the Earth below, and thought.

Eye wunder wot wud appen
iv eye aimd dis laizer raigun
att datt planit....
    an den pult der trigger?

It was 5 past 7 on the planet Earth.
(Skip was busy in his tent.)
The scouts were trying to light
fires by rubbing sticks together.
Darren and Garry had decided that
it was impossible and were just
about to give up when . . .

SKIP'S TENT

Be easier if one
stick was a match.

Skip said,
'Ray?..snuffle..er..yawn..who?'
So they told him again.

And he said,
'Oh well, I suppose I shall have
to get up.'
But when he saw that they *had*
lit a fire, he said.

Well done lads. What did I tell you.
All it takes is a bit of ingenuity.
Tonight we'll cook sausages, and
sing songs around the old camp fire.

The 3rd Balsawood Road Scout troop
were feeling happy and content.
They'd scoffed a load of sausages
and were now sitting around the
old camp fire, deciding what song
to sing first . . .

when Garry Wimbush saw
something strange.

Hey Skip. Look!
What's that in the sky?

Skip knew what it was.

It's only a shooting-star, Garry. A shooting-star is really just a tiny meteorite, which burns up as it enters the Earth's atmosphere. Nothing to get excited about.

But he was wrong.

For in another part of the woods
an alien space monster was setting
about the conquest of the Earth.

IT WAS BLACKBANK WOOD.

IT WAS A WOGGLE.

But Grott was not a particularly
clever alien . . .

Nor was he particularly brave . . .

And he was beginning to wish he'd
never come to this particular planet,
when he heard a strange sound.
A familiar sound.
Alien voices singing.
Singing in Grobblewockian!
And what they were singing was

On hearing this, Grott's alien heart
leapt with alien joy and he ran on
his little alien legs as fast as he
could towards the sound –
where he found . . .

Now if there's one thing that a Grobblewockian loves more than conquering a planet or destroying a civilisation – it's a sausage. And so it was with a happy heart that Alien Grott leapt into the middle of the camp-fire circle and said:

Unfortunately neither Skip or the scouts realized that this meant 'Thank you very much, I'd love a sausage.'
They thought it simply meant 'Arghleegh-soggle-wog!'
And decided that the most appropriate reply was:

Ging-Gang goolie goolie...
"RUN for it!!"

Now Skip had read many books on scouting but had never come across any instructions as to what to do if an alien space monster invades your campsite.

Darren Twigg read the Beano so he knew exactly what to do —

NB. 'SCRAGGING" - is a word used to describe what happens when a lot of small boys jump on top of one large grown-up person — or alien.

FOR EXAMPLE :-

If these small boys were to SCRAGG this particular alien..

This is what would happen

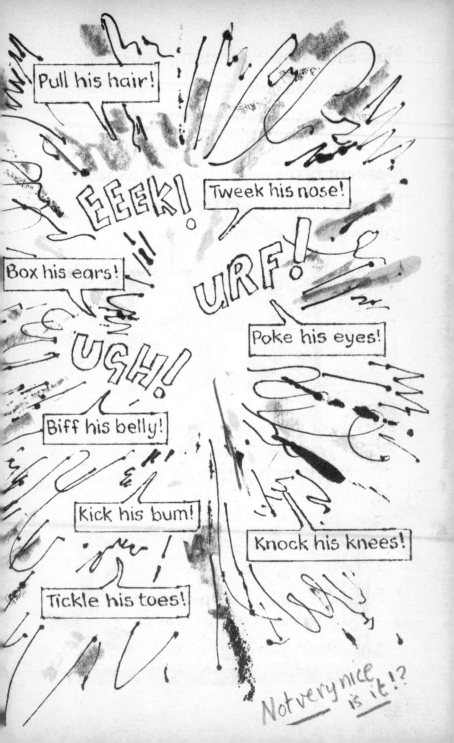

'No,' said Skip. 'That's not very nice.'
Then he said

We are not hooligans, ruffians or thugs.
<u>We are scouts</u>
We must never forget the old scout motto.

THE OLD SCOUT MOTTO

◇ A scout ◇
smiles AND whistles
under all difficulties

19 18

And so –

And –

Then –

Grott didn't know what to do
either. He was quite used to people
running off when they saw him,
shouting things like – ELP! ELP!!
and – YUCK! INTIT MON STRUSS!
But all this smiling and whistling,
he didn't understand.

He knew there was something he
was supposed to do about things
he didn't understand.
He tried to think what it was –

Meanwhile Skip had remembered
an old saying –

> He who smiles and runs away
> lives to smile another day

He gathered the scouts around him
and said:

Listen carefully.
I've got a plan.

But Garry Wimbush was *not* listening.
He had <u>seen</u> something.
And without thinking twice
Garry Wimbush marched up to the
huge ugly alien space monster
and said:

Hey Bonehead!
Where d'you find
that woggle?

Now what Garry Wimbush didn't know
was that –
'Hey Bonehead! Where d'you find
that woggle?'
was Grobblewockian for
'Grey phone-bed! Bear blue fly and
cat-goggles?'.
Grott, not surprisingly, didn't
understand what this meant.
He knew there was something he was
supposed to do about things he
didn't understand. He tried to
think what it was.

Then he remembered!
The old Grobblewockian motto . . .

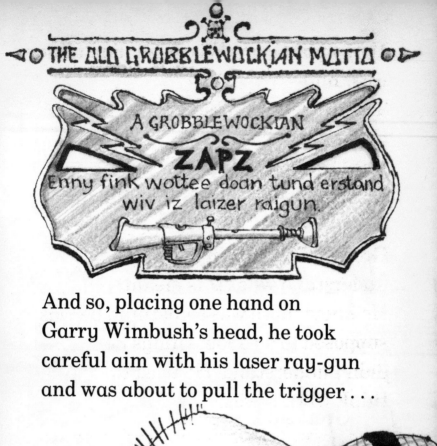

THE OLD GROBBLEWOCKIAN MOTTO

A GROBBLEWOCKIAN
ZAPZ
Enny fink wottee doan tund erstand
wiv iz laizer raigun.

And so, placing one hand on
Garry Wimbush's head, he took
careful aim with his laser ray-gun
and was about to pull the trigger . . .

when . . .

. . . he saw something on Garry's shirt and said:

Garry said: ➘

Grott said: ➘

'Where's the rest of your troop?'
said Garry.
'Doan tund erstand,' said Grott.
'Doing handstands?' said Garry.
'Wotsa hats tand?' said Grott.

I could go on to tell you
all the other things that Garry
and Grott said to each other —
But you wouldn't understand.

No. Really — you wouldn't!

You see, after a while neither
Garry nor Grott knew what
they were saying either.

The important thing to remember
is this :—

Sometimes it's not WHAT
people say to each other
that makes them become friends

Sometimes it's simply HOW
they say it.

AND SO ⟶

By morning, Garry and Grott, Skip,
and the rest of the troop
were smiling and laughing
and slapping each other on the back
and saying things like –
'Ging-gang jamboree?'
'Oh, Grobble-woggle reef-knot
and dib dib dib!'
Skip noticed that Grott kept
repeating one particular word . . .

Bajiz!?

and he said:

If you learn to be
a good Boy Scout
you can have <u>lots</u> of badges.

And so...

Over the next few days,
Grott learned how to camp . . .

How to use a compass . . .

He was made chief fire-lighter . . .

and he was awarded . . .

61

He was so happy he quite forgot
about his mission . . .
until Wednesday night when
he remembered,

Iv yer knot back bye Wenz-dee,
wheel go ome wivout yoo.

And so,
with sadness in his heart,
he crept quietly back to where
his scout-ship was hidden and . . .

Next morning, at breakfast,
Darren Twigg said:

> Hey Skip. You know shooting-stars, like the one we saw the other night. Do they ever go back up the other way?

To which Skip replied:

> Darren Twigg, you haven't got the brain of a gnat!

> It wasn't on the list.

And that is how Garry Wimbush
and the 3rd Balsawood Rd scouts
saved the world from an
alien invasion.

And that is why on the planet Grob,
trillions of billions of squillions
of miles away from Earth, there now
lives a race of alien space monsters
who no longer go around the galaxy
destroying civilisations.

Now, when they land on a planet,
they spend their time building
tree-huts, lighting camp fires, and
making really useful things out of
wood, rope and yogurt cartons.
So . . . .

THE END